Ernest McGaffey

Poems of Gun and Rod

Ernest McGaffey

Poems of Gun and Rod

ISBN/EAN: 9783337021658

Printed in Europe, USA, Canada, Australia, Japan

Cover: Foto ©Andreas Hilbeck / pixelio.de

More available books at **www.hansebooks.com**

POEMS OF GUN AND ROD

POEMS OF GUN AND ROD

BY ERNEST McGAFFEY

ILLUSTRATED BY HERBERT E. BUTLER

CHARLES SCRIBNER'S SONS
NEW YORK, 1892

GREETING

DEAR comrades of my happy out-door days,
These halting rhymes, that from my heart I send,
With midnight stars and flakes of dawning blend
With morning's gray and sunset's steady blaze ;
And up through marshy flats and wooded ways
Where tall oaks rise, and rustling rushes bend,
Passes the form of many an old-time friend
Who trod with me the field and forest maze
From dawn to dusk ; I count them as they pass,
And leaps my blood again as one by one
The old days rise, while Nature's Circe-strain,
That lures men on 'mid sun and wind and rain,
Comes back to me o'er harps of tangled grass
And sets me dreaming of the rod and gun.

CONTENTS

LIST OF ILLUSTRATIONS

The Gun

THE GUN

With perfect lines from butt to sight,
  Damascus barrels, twelve in gauge
That shine within like mirrors bright,
  A triumph of this latter age;
Gnarled walnut wood the solid stock,
  And smoother than your finger-nail
Extension rib, rebounding lock,
  And balanced like a truthful scale.

No fine engraving tracery shown
  On locks or barrels for the vain,
A weapon for its worth alone,
  A beauty, yet severely plain;
Top-snap the action, as you see,
  And corrugated buck-horn tip,
As finished as an arm should be
  From muzzle through to pistol-grip.

A trusty comrade, this old gun,
  And certain, if you hold it right,

To drop the jack-snipe one by one
  Or stop a partridge in his flight—
To bring to earth the woodcock where
  In lowland covert out he springs,
Or send far up in crispy air
  The death-hail, where the wild-goose wings.

Let Folly's votaries fill her train,
  And chirping poets feebly rhyme ;
In dingy holes for worldly gain
  Let stooping dullards spend their prime ;
Let hermits prose in doleful moods,
And book-worms in dry volumes delve,
  Give me the rivers, lakes, and woods,
My freedom and the " Number Twelve."

AS THE DAY BREAKS

I PRAY you, what's asleep?
  The lily-pads, and riffles, and the reeds ;
No longer inward do the waters creep
  No longer outwardly their force recedes,
And widowed night, in blackness wide and deep,
  Resumes her weeds.

I pray you, what's awake ?
  A host of stars, the long, long milky way
That stretches out, a glistening silver flake,
  All glorious beneath the moon's cold ray,
And myriad reflections on the lake
  Where star-gleams lay.

I pray you, what's astir ?
  Why, naught but rustling leaves. dry, sere, and brown :
The East's broad gates are yet a dusky blur
  And star-gems twinkle in fair Luna's crown,
And minor chords of wailing winds that were
  Die slowly down.

I pray you, what's o'clock.?
　　Nay! who shall answer that but gray-stoled dawn?
See, how from out the shadows looms yon rock
　　Like some great figure on a canvas drawn;
And heard you not the crowing of the cock?
　　The night is gone.

"Mark."

"MARK"

THE heavy mists have crept away,
    Heavily swims the sun,
And dim in mystic cloudlands gray,
    The stars fade one by one ;
Out of the dusk enveloping
    Come marsh and sky and tree,
Where erst has rested night's dark ring
    Over the Kankakee.

" Mark right ! "   Afar and faint outlined
    A flock of mallards fly,
We crouch within the reedy blind
    Instantly at the cry.
" Mark left ! "   We peer through wild rice-blades
    And distant shadows see,
A wedge-shaped phalanx from the shades
    Of far-off Kankakee.

" Mark overhead ! "   A canvasback !
    " Mark !   Mark ! "   A bunch of teal !

And swiftly on each flying track
    Follows the shot-gun's peal ;
Thus rings that call, till twilight's tide
    Rolls in like some gray sea,
And whippoorwills complain beside
    The lonely Kankakee.

SPRING

SOMEWHAT of broken clouds edge-tipped with blue,
   Scattered and listless in the ashen sky,
   A sound of happy waters flowing by,
And little blades of grass shy peeping through
The old earth's crevices ; and starting new
   Are swelling buds upon the many boughs ;
   Long wakes of black behind advancing ploughs,
And plough-shares misty with the morning dew.

Soon, soon, indeed, the couriers will bring
   Swift tidings of the joyous days to come,
   When Nature's heart, but yet so lately numb,
Shall beat again, and birds will once more sing ;
No more shall wintry arrows pierce and sting
   For far from where the chiding north-wind frets,
   Here in a nook are dainty violets,
The meek and blue-eyed harbingers of spring.

MORNING IN THE HILLS

FAINT streaks of light in the far-down east
   Outlined by an unseen pencil,
The artist hand of the dawn's high priest
   Who spreads o'er a shadowed stencil
The silver hues of the morning's wings,
   The dusk and the darkness flaking,
While the old earth sighs, and the pine-top sings,
   " Awake ! for the day is breaking."

The gray squir'l barks, for the woods are still,
   And the silence makes him braver,
And he sees the sun behind the hill
   Where the shadows twist and waver ;

The gray squir'l watches the dead leaves whirl,
   That the sun no more shall nourish,
High on a branch with his tail a-curl
   Like a writing-master's flourish.

The partridge drums on an old dry log
   A haunt of worm and cricket,
Down near the edge of a cranberry bog,
   Close by a white birch thicket ;
And at times the reverberation floats
   Through the air so round and mellow,
That it sounds as sweet as the basso notes
   Of a maestro's violoncello.

The gray squir'l barks, and the partridge drums,
   And the sunlight follows faster,
And over the pines the wind-god comes
   With the touch of an untaught master,
And he strikes the chords from a maze of limbs
   That glitter with frost-lace hoary,
While eastward now as the darkness dims
Is the sun in a sea of glory.

"Over the Decoys"

LONE lies the tawny marsh, and lily pads,
All crisped and wrinkled by the autumn sun,
Swim lazily along the sighing reeds ;
The strident reeds, that bar the passage-way,
Where wanders past the lost and wailing breeze
Over the gray, wan deserts of the dawn,
Striking the frets of intertwining stems
That rustle into weirdest music there.

And ruddily against the rising sun
The ever-restless waters ripple up,
Prying amid the rushes, and again,
Upon the roots of dwarfish willow stubs,
Lapping and lapping like a thirsty hound :

And in an open space beyond the reeds,
Riding like corks the little ruffled waves,
Decoys are seen, those fateful wooden lures
That draw the passing ducks from cloudy heights
Down, down, and down, until the sportsman's aim
Sends consternation to their scattered ranks.

And at the edges of the cat-tails tall,
Among the rushes and the spatter-dock,
A hunter waits, all watchful, in the " blind,"
Whose rough, artistic tracing seems to be,
With all its tangled drapery of reeds,
Wild rice, and grass, and leaning willow-branch,
Like elfin work of nature and the winds.

Mark ! far adown the distant line of trees
A narrow dusky ribbon is revealed,
That nearer comes, and as it comes unfolds,
And shows in all their symmetry of form
A flock of ducks outlined upon the sky,
Curving and wheeling in the morning light.

And as they near the hunter's ambuscade
They turn, they stoop, while he with muscles set,
And tense as steel, and eager-shining eyes
Sits like a stone, his gun within his hands ;
The winds are hushed.   Ah ! what a picture that—
The blue-bills settling to the still decoys.

TWILIGHT

Down in the edge of a tamarack swamp
  A rabbit lay in his burrow,
And he heard the elves of Boreas romp
  Through the woods and field and furrow ;
And out in the dusk the glow-worm lit
  His lamp in the misty gloaming,
And the night-hawks over the trees would flit
  And out through the night go roaming.

A cricket chirped on a sassafras limb,
  A tree-toad piped on a willow,
And the full moon's circle lay all dim
  Reclined on a cloudy pillow ;
A whippoorwill in the distance cried,
  And a few lone star-gleams twinkled,
While drifting over the meadow wide
  The cow-bells clanged and tinkled.

Like the changing folds of an ancient loom
  That the eye and mind perplexes,

A bat criss-crossed in the deepening gloom
    And marked aërial X's ;
While up from the edge of a shallow bog,
    With its moss-banks soft and porous,
Came the sound of minstrels all agog—
    The bull-frogs' opening chorus.

The mist grew clear, and the clouds grew bright,
    And the silence crisp and crisper,
And the trailing folds of the robe of night
    Came soft as a ghostly whisper ;
And out in the skies the full moon sailed
    With the stars to all attend her,
And the pearl-gray tints of the twilight failed
    In night's Cimmerian splendor.

A SWALLOW

I sing you a song of a swallow
  With a purple breast and buoyant wings,
  Curving down where the south wind springs
From out of a grassy hollow.

From out of a sylvan hollow—
  And the swift wings swerve where water sleeps,
  And up from the depths a ripple leaps
At the dip of a darting swallow.

At the touch of a mad-cap swallow—
  And his rhythmic sweep of motion brings
  The sudden sense of a soul on wings,
That leads where I long to follow.

JACK-SNIPE

THE wild rice dips, the wild rice bends
And rustles in the breeze,
As down the marsh the west wind sends
Its message from the trees ;
   The wild rice stalks together mass
   As overhead the jack-snipe pass,
And higher still the shining moon
Sails on through night's deep noon.

The wild rice bends, the wild rice dips
And whispers soft and low ;
Like greyhounds loosed from straining slips,
O'erhead the jack-snipe go ;
   Above dead limbs, gaunt, naked spars,
   And underneath a sea of stars,
Pale, pallid stars and argent moon
That make of midnight noon.

The wild rice dips, the wild rice bends,
As through the starry night

With sharp-set wing the jack-snipe trends
His migratory flight;
  The wild rice shivers, as with cold,
  And in the heavens, old, so old,
Dims down the heights the waning moon
And fades the night's fair noon.

SUMMER

A LANGUOROUS, heavy air, with bees a-tune
   O'er basswood-blossoms and the clover-tops ;
   A drowsy atmosphere that reels and drops
Steeped to the core in this red wine of June,
The breathless splendor of a mellow noon,
   Where grasses droop beneath the fervent heat
   And sun-flakes come, on golden-sandalled feet,
To kiss the flowers till they fall a-swoon.

Naught but the stillness of the amber air,
   No song of bird, no echo of a song.
   The slothful river slowly dreams along
Where lily-cups are floating lily fair ;
A strange and balmy muteness everywhere,
   Filling the universe with silence deep,
   For Summer's hand has rocked the world to sleep
And smoothed the wrinkles in her brow of care.

DAYBREAK on the MARSH

Far to the west the heavy timber stands
In purple bands,
And in the east the blossoming day expands
    As through the clouds the sun-streaks break and flit,
    While bit by bit
Creeps forth the earth to warm herself by morning's
    smouldering brands.

Emancipated from the night's dark frown
Stand marshes brown,
And shrill autumnal gusts come sweeping down
    Holding within their clutches captive leaves
    From branching eaves,
With red and russet blazoned smooth, reft from October's
    crown.

And from the amber waters upward spring,
With dripping wing,
The waterfowl and circle, wandering ;
   In airy journeys swerving up on high
   As through the sky
They turn their course to northward, where polar breezes
     sting.

And far and near, as onward still they go,
From coverts low,
White puffs of smoke, unfolding, faintly show
   Where in his " blind " the hidden sportsman lies,
   With watchful eyes,
Sending his bright flame-signals up through dawn's dull-
     steeping glow.

THE CALL OF THE UPLAND PLOVER

On a wide, lone waste of prairie cover,
Studded with flowers here and there,
Where shadows fall as the clouds drift over,
And the land lies silent everywhere—
All suddenly, sharply, comes a calling
In flute-like notes from the far sky falling.

Where never a sound else greets the comer,
This call goes drifting past alone,
Slow sinking down through a sea of summer
And over the wind-swept prairie blown,
Where the long, rich grass bends low and closes
Over the thorn-clad red wild roses.

A bird's clear call in a rippling whistle,
Floating by on the fitful breeze,
Light as the down from a shattered thistle,
Sweet as the murmur of swaying trees ;
The fresh, free cry of a prairie rover,
The uncaged call of an upland plover.,

Flushed

FLUSHED

THICK coverts in the island bogs,
With here and there dark, shallow pools,
Where wriggling tadpoles swim in schools
Around the black, half-sunken logs;
And with its limbs like gaunt-hewn hands
A sycamore's huge, knotted trunk,
As some old, shorn, and wrinkled monk,
Solemnly in the silence stands.

A rustling where the cover lays,
A soft step pattering in the brake—
A form that makes the alders shake
Threading along in winding ways,
And then within a brushy place
From out an opening appears,
With great brown eyes and silken ears.
An eager water-spaniel's face.

He takes one step, when outward springs
A bird whose arrowy, agile flight

Seems as a sudden flash of light
Borne upward on mercurial wings;
The hanging brush an instant parts,
Shrill sounds a whistle of surprise,
And, meteor-like, before his eyes
Up through the trees a woodcock darts.

THE YELLOW-HAMMER

WHITE shreds of cloud, like foamy surf,
  Horizonward float past,
And slantwise on the emerald turf
  Their lengthened shadows cast.
While dark against the morning sun,
Whose ruddy creepers upward run,
Silent along the silent sky
The brown cow-blackbirds fly.

And piercing out as trumpet shrill
  The flicker's challenge breaks
From out the oaks which crown a hill
  That overlooks the lakes ;
A long-drawn chattering cry elate,
And then from his expectant mate
A faint-heard answering cry replies
From some far wooded rise.

And then across an open place
  Between the serried trees,

High up in sun-surrounded space,
   A golden shadow flees,
In curves that rise and curves that dip
As graceful as a courtesying ship,
With measured stroke of pinions bright
That marks the flicker's flight.

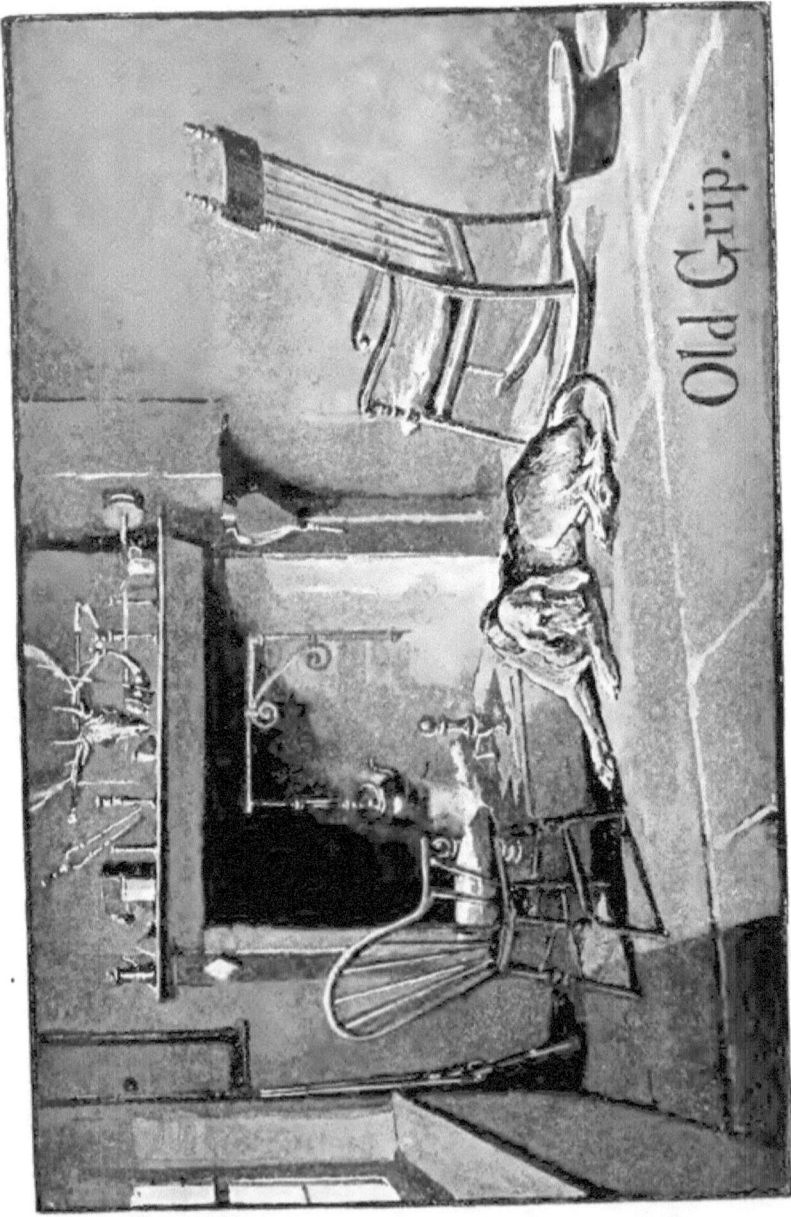

Old Grip.

OLD GRIP

HE dreams beside the chimney's base
There in his snug, accustomed place ;
The kettle sings upon the crane
And on the window clinks the rain,
While bogies from the chimney tall
Throw shadow-shafts along the wall ;
Yet recks he not of sight or sound—
Old Grip, the rabbit hound.

How strong he is, from brawny hips
Up to his tawny, wrinkled lips ;
From muzzle to the velvet flank
From chest to barrel, neck to shank ;
How graceful, and how lithe and fleet,
Why, when he runs, his nimble feet
Seem in their flight to skim the ground—
Old Grip, the rabbit hound.

The hickory back-log glows and shines,
And in his sleep the old dog whines ;

Again he roams among the trees
And "molly cottontail" he sees;
Then instantly away, away,
While ring the woods with mellow bay,
Clearing the fences at a bound—
Old Grip, the rabbit hound.

The faithfulness you seek from friends
In hollow phrase begins and ends;
The love of woman that you crave
Breaks like the bubble on a wave;
The world, that grim old pedagogue,
Has taught me to respect a dog,
For faith and love can aye be found
In Grip. the rabbit hound.

THE WIND IN THE TREES

THE camp-fire smoulders, the charred fagots darkle,
As night from her canopy reigns;
The glow-worms alternately vanish and sparkle
Weird swamp-light that waxes and wanes,
And aloft, like a murmur of myriad bees
　　Is the wind in the trees.

I lie on my blanket, a saddle my pillow,
And watch the pale crescent on high;
Each pine-top sways down like a slim wand of willow
As gathering breezes go by,
While the music I hear as I rest at my ease
　　Is the wind in the trees.

The hound at my feet crouches low near an ember
And harks to the camp-kettle's croon,
The ash-heaps have ridged like the snows of December
And cold in the rays of the moon,
While rising and falling in lulling degrees
　　Is the wind in the trees.

A rustling of leaves and a creaking of branches,
A herald of midnight borne fast ;
A rush, as of loosened and mad avalanches,
And peace when the tumult has passed ;
An ebb and a flow of aërial seas—
    Is the wind in the trees.

There's a throb in my heart and a mist on my lashes
As darkness around me is thrown,
While the world fades away like the crumbling of ashes
As I wander through mazes unknown ;
And above me, wild songs in Æolian keys,
    Is the wind in the trees.

Gone Away

GONE AWAY

HILL, meadow, dale, and rustling woods,
  And overhead are sharp cloud-lines
Etched on the skyey solitudes ;
  A fresh wind blown from scented pines,
A clash of hoofs, a motley rout
  Crossing the road in bright array ;
Hark to that sudden, eager shout—
  " Gone away, away ; gone away ! "

Then o'er the country-side resounds
  The wild, weird music of the chase ;
Far, far ahead the gallant hounds
  Together running, lead the race ;
And after them the hunters pass
  Like arrows through the morning gray ;
Hark ! quivering o'er the trampled grass—
  " Gone away, away ; gone away ! "

Through the sheep-pasture runs the fox,
  Steals, wraith-like, 'mid the thickets dense,

Trips nimbly over logs and rocks
   Then glides along an old rail fence,
And faintly sounds within his ears
   The leading dog's melodious bay ;
The opening cry no more he hears—
   " Gone away, away ; gone away ! "

The noise dies out, and wood-birds call
   From quiet, leafy coverts dim,
And acorns from the oak-trees tall
   Drop, plummet-like, from topmost limb ;
All now is hushed, sweet silence reigns
   And yet an echo seems to say,
Soft whispering through the fields and lanes—
   " Gone away, away ; gone away ! "

AT THE THRESHOLD

Prone on her face at Autumn's feet,
Where August and September meet,
Lies Summer, and complaining grieves
The changing tints of all her leaves,
The gathering bloom upon the rye,
The darker purple in the sky ;
While at the threshold waiting stands
A messenger from other lands.

No more bright clover tufts shall nod
Above the warm, sunshiny sod,
Along the streams and o'er the hills
A russet tide its force instils ;
Brown-vestured monks are all the trees,
And gone the hum of wandering bees ;
While through the misty woodlands dusk
Float pungent odors, myrrh and musk.

Oh, Summer ! still thy splendor fades,
As deeper grow autumnal shades,

And still the air an incense yields
Slow rising from the stubble-fields,
Flames red the sumach by the wall
More clearly sweet the waters call,
And by the road where travellers plod
Spring feathery spires of golden-rod.

For thee no more shall roses blow,
Nor odorous south winds come and go,
Before thy sight no more shall pass
Cloud-shadows o'er the meadow grass,
Gone are the signs of summer drouth
With swift-winged swallows hurrying south,
For shadowed forth, with sun-browned hands,
Old Autumn at the threshold stands.

Quail.

QUAIL

Down near the timber, at a corn-field's edge,
Where airy thistle seeds
Sail back and forth where each air-current leads,
Close by the corner of a tangled hedge,
A dog stands firm, half-hidden in the weeds
And listens, yet no warning whistle heeds.

Patient he waits ; his attitude the same
As when, all unaware,
While rummaging and snuffing here and there
The scent came suddenly of lurking game ;
His wrinkled nose sniffs at the tainted air
And in the maze his sharp eyes sideways stare.

Around the hedge his master slowly walks,
And walking, tramps and stirs
In grassy covert, briars, weeds, and burrs,
Brushing the gossamers from thistle stalks ;
Then sees the dog, steps to the matted furze
An instant more, and up the bevy whirrs.

Over the scrub, with buzzing wings it goes
And scatters in affright;
Up to his shoulder, as he marks the flight,
The hunter instantly his shot-gun throws,
And feathers slow are drifting, brown and white,
As ring the detonations left and right.

IN THE TAMARACKS

Slim, feathery-shafted trees that lift
   Their cone-like branchings dry,
Where streaks of sunlight slowly sift
And filter down each narrow rift
   To where the mosses lie ;
And brambles, logs, and matted shoots
Stretch, cross, and twist round gnarly roots.

And there a wandering footstep sounds,
   Slow moving here and there
Over the yielding, spongy mounds
And circling in recurring rounds
   And out through spaces bare ;
Then all at once the noises sink,
While slides the sun through many a chink.

Then a gay blue-jay shrilly calls,
   And round a rotten stump
A garter-snake, all glistening, crawls,

And, hark ! again the footstep falls
  Beside a brushy clump ;
Rings a report, and through the limbs
An old cock partridge swiftly skims.

My Ancient
Hunting Coat

MY ANCIENT HUNTING-COAT

An old brown garment, patched and weather-worn,
  With pockets numberless on every side,
Long, ragged rents, by envious briars torn,
  And darkened spots in divers places dyed;
Faint streaks of yellow here and there descried,
  And ravelled edges by the thickets shorn,
A rough, stanch coat thro' storm and sunshine tried
  And over many a mile of field and prairie borne.

Discolored by the sleet and driving rain
  And faded by the burning autumn sun,
The texture firm, with interwoven grain
  Within its russet threads, though closely spun
Shows what the gnáwing teeth of time have done;
  On the right shoulder is a smooth, wide stain
That marks the place where, shiftingly, the gun
  Has in my old-time out-door wanderings often lain.

Here is some plumage from a pheasant's crest,
  And here are traces of a rabbit's fur,

And in this corner, hidden with the rest,
  Clings to the cloth a prickly cockle-bur
That pierces suddenly and like a spur ;
  And in this upper pocket close are pressed
Old sprays of sumach, full of woodsy myrrh
  And various feathers, too, in motley colors drest.

And these bring pictures to my dreaming eyes
  Of river, woodland, marsh, and stubble-field,
As by-gone days, like ghosts forgotten rise
  And olden memories are again unsealed ;
Like legends carven on an antique shield
  These days come back and woo in dear disguise
While Nature waits, in loveliness revealed,
  Under a still, rapt glory of far unshadowed skies.

THE BLUE-JAY

THE blackbird whistles in early spring,
And the bob'link's notes o'er the meadows ring;
The swallows twitter from the ivied wall
But the blue-jay comes in the fall.

The robin pipes when the sunlight shines,
And the oriole sings in the tangled vines;
In summer thickets the cat-birds call
But the blue-jay comes in the fall.

The wild canary likes the weather warm,
And the brown thrush chants after each June storm;
When the green leaves turn they will vanish all
But the blue-jay comes in the fall.

These sun-nourished songsters, let them go,
For they dare not face one flake of snow;
The bare trees herald the winter's thrall
But the blue-jay comes in the fall.

And down in the woods I heard his cry,
And his bright blue wings went flashing by ;
December waits with an icy pall
But the blue-jay comes in the fall.

"A POINT"

A "POINT"

By rude November's hands the woods are shorn,
 And dead leaves whirl in gusty eddies round ;
And by an old rail fence a field of corn
 Sways, snaps, and rustles with a creaking sound
As dry husks break and flutter to the ground ;
 While sigh the winds in melody forlorn,
And crisp, thick grass, by russet autumn browned,
 Waves in the cool tide floating o'er the morn.

Deep in a thorny patch that skirts the fence
 Are huddled close a bevy of shy quail,
Where the wide thicket reaches brown and dense,
 Along a slope that crowns the narrow swale ;
All cosily they nestle 'neath a veil
 Of briars and of thistle-stalks, from whence
Wee ships of gossamer spread snowy sail,
 And cobwebs stretch in fairy tether tense.

Lo ! a light footstep, and a dog draws nigh,
 Then pauses, rigid, as if carved of stone,

And quick excitement lights his eager eye,
   As straight ahead his piercing glance is thrown ;
The well-known scent across his pathway blown
   Fills his keen nostrils as it passes by,
And tells him that among the briars prone,
   And out of sight, the bright-eyed bevy lie.

IN AUTUMN WOODS

CRISP-RUSTLING leaves in scattered lines
Under the bare, deserted trees ;
Dead branches stripped of every leaf,
And sombre winds that tell their grief
Through shadowy vistas such as these,
Hung here and there with russet vines ;
Gone all the colors June once bore
And all that Indian-summer wore,
While in the creek's smooth pools below
The waters dark and darker glow,
    In Autumn Woods.

Sweet, silent hushes in these aisles,
Filled with the breath of lasting calm ;
Æolian echoes, vaguely strange,
That whisper of eventful change,
While cleaving through the misty balm
A wandering sunbeam softly smiles ;
Here lurks amid the arches rude

The gray old ghost of solitude,
And here along the lonely path
Fades out the summer's aftermath,
In Autumn Woods.

A Prairie Rover.

H.E. BUTLER

A PRAIRIE ROVER

ALONG a line of timber lies the lake,
A liquid floor,
And wailing croons November's eerie voice
Beside the shore ;
The lily-pads, like sleeping faces, lie
Upon a bed
Of dimpled waters, shadow-crossed and lone,
And overhead,
All meteor-like across the russet sky,
A bunch of teal come sailing swiftly by.

And in their airy wake, and gaining fast
With lightning speed, a dark bird whizzes past.

One whirling curve pursuers and pursued
Together make,
Then downward stoops the scattered line of ducks
Toward the lake ;
But as they near the refuge waiting there,
The duck-hawk springs,

Cutting the trembling air at one quick swoop
With rustling wings,
And o'er the prairie, floating soft and white,
Are feather-signs that mark the duck-hawk's flight.

SUMACH

COARSE-GRAINED and harsh the slender stalks
Of wayside sumach stand,
And each lithe branch uplifted seems
As some cup-bearer, tanned,
Who holds to Autumn's lips divine
A goblet of sun-tinted wine
With mute, adoring hand.

And deeply to the very lees
The russet goddess drains
These jewelled cups that erst were filled
From Summer's glowing veins—
Red draughts that hold the subtle sense
Of pungent sylvan frankincense
And misty later rains.

Then, like some alchemy of old,
The magic ichor flies
From pulse to heart, and rising lends
New glory to her eyes,

Where shadowy fire an instant leaps
As lightning from a cloud that sleeps
Fast moored in stormy skies.

And blithely as she passes on
Sound Autumn's chariot-wheels,
As gliding through her being swift,
The sumach's life she feels;
While over all the landscape brown
A flood of sunlight rushes down
And baffled winter kneels.

"HARD HIT"

H.C.BUTLER

" HARD HIT "

Grim on a topmost branch he stood,
   All statue-like, against the sky,
The breath of Autumn filled the wood
   And slumbrous clouds swam far on high.

Then, whip-like, came a rifle-shot—
   How sinister its challenge sang !
And with his death-wound fairly got
   Into the air the old hawk sprang.

One stroke his wings made ere he swerved
   High o'er the shadow-haunted dell,
One blow with talons outward curved,
   Then, sudden as he leaped, he fell.

AUTUMN

A CORN-FIELD stretching to the woods below,
Where corn-husks crack and, breaking up, unfold
The grains of corn in many a tempting row,
With Nature's stamp upon the virgin gold ;
Great yellow pumpkins on the fertile mould,
And vines slow-spreading through the spaces dim,
While over all a whispered vesper hymn
Drifts from the edges of the forest old.

And there, arrayed in burnished armor brown,
Tall, solemn oaks, like giant warriors rise,
And through the hazy vistas dropping down,
Come buoyant leaves, in red and russet dyes,
Above the trees a lone crow slowly flies
Winging his flight toward the dying sun,
While Autumn, like a sweet-faced, holy nun,
Shades with a trembling hand her sad brown eyes.

RED AND BROWN

The sumach's flaming colors rise beside the old stone
　wall
　And hazel-bushes, sunshine-browned, are whispering
　　in the breeze,
While through the woods on every side is heard the
　crackling fall
　Of ripened nuts slow falling from the swaying hickory-
　　trees.

Upon a gnarled and new-cut stump beneath the sturdy
　oaks
　A spider, running back and forth, a fairy circle
　　weaves—
A silver wheel, whose glistening hub and filmy maze of
　spokes
　Is stretched across the splinters in the shadow of the
　　leaves.

The velvet moss on ancient logs is fading into gray;
　A fox-squirrel runs across the leaves, that rustle as he
　　leaps,

And through the trees the sunlight falls and slowly melts
    away,
  Where round a bend in darkling curves the pulsing
    water sweeps.

Low, sweet and low, and liquidly, the creek's faint
    echoes call,
  While on its amber current float the oak-leaves crisp
    and brown,
And all day long, as winds dance past across the tree-tops
    tall,
  From branches bare the hickory-nuts come rattling
    slowly down.

The

Twelve-tined

Buck.

THE TWELVE-TINED BUCK

THE mist rose out of the valley,
   The mist climbed up from the lake,
And a musk-rat's course in the water
   Spread out in a glimmering wake.

The red sun's edge came peeping
   O'er the top of a far-off hill,
The winds lay furled in the floating clouds
   And the leaves and the grass were still.

But over the pines and cedars
   Re-echoed a distant horn,
And a hound's faint bay chimed with it
   In the hush of the waking morn.

And then from a balsam thicket
   Came the sound of a sudden crash,
And a twelve-tined buck sprang out and stood
   By the side of a quaking ash.

His horns were brown as the Autumn,
　And his hoofs like jasper shone,
And his dark eyes gleamed in the dawning
　As he snuffed the breeze alone.

And then as the gathering echoes
　Brought up the hounds' deep cry,
He passed like a steel-gray shadow
　And scattered the pine-cones dry.

And down through the tall pine timber,
　As an arrow will cut its way,
He fled to the quickening clamor
　Of the hounds with their mellow bay.

The partridge flew from the pine-top
　As the twelve-tined buck went by,
And the chipmunk dived in a knot-hole smooth
　And closed his glittering eye.

And a black-snake slid from his coiling
　And deeper in shadows crept,
And a great white owl, disturbed on high,
　Called once, and then he slept.

But out from the shade and shadow,
　And down through the woods apace,

Came the deer with the dogs pursuing,
  And out through an open space.

And there for a fateful instant
  The crack of a rifle came,
A puff of smoke in the russet air,
  Death-tipped with a dart of flame.

But over the buck's broad antlers
  The wandering bullet flew,
And into the tangled copses
  He plunged and battled through.

While still on the trail came floating,
  As he fled with his mighty bounds,
The deep, relentless baying
  Of the first of the foremost hounds.

So he turned to the sleeping water
  Edged round with spongy moss,
And leaped in the dimpling ripples
  And bravely swam across,

Where a long, low island stretching,
  In the midst of the lonely lake,
Held bog and fern, and a haven
  Of shadowy, wildest brake.

And into its far recesses
  He dropped like a wind-tossed waif,
And a deer-hound whined on the shore he left,
  But the twelve-tined buck was safe.

PAN

By the wandering river
Forever,
Where restless waters ran,
Would the reeds croon low
When the winds did blow,
Under the touch of Pan,
Great Pan,
Who played where the ripples ran.

At the edge of the river,
Oh! never
As yet surpassed by man,
From the reed-bed floats
Those musical notes
Fresh from the lips of Pan,
God Pan,
So far from the haunts of man.

None by the dreaming river
Shall ever

6

His face or figure scan,
Yet they all may hear
A melody clear,
The rhythmic runes of Pan,
Gray Pan,
In the wilds remote from man.

ÆOLIAN ECHOES

Nay, then, for trifles rude as these
　Shall Orpheus sweep the vibrant strings:
" A squirrel's brush, a sumach bough,"
　" A partridge and a jay-bird's wings."

I see the dull December woods
　Most darkly wrapped in sombre hue,
And lightly through their leafless tops
　The jay-bird flits—a patch of blue.

And where among the branches bare
　The waves of morning rise and fall,
All querulous and shrill resounds
　The wandering jay-bird's woodland call.

A hickory-tree among the oaks
  An instant in the stillness swings,
As from the slender topmost limbs
  A hurrying squirrel outward springs.

And down a gnarled and ancient oak
  With agile leaps the space he clears,
Near to a hole his gay brush flaunts
  One moment, then he disappears.

A waste of leaves all crisp and brown,
  And briars where the cobweb clings ;
Old logs, a brush-pile here and there,
  And all at once a whirr of wings.

As from a hazel-thicket dense
  Near to a rolling wooded rise,
With rustling noise of pinions broad,
  Swift through the trees a partridge flies.

A scarlet tinge that dyes the west,
  Cloud-ships beneath with ruddy prows,
And redder still, yet darkly red,
  I see the glowing sumach boughs.

Their clustered shapes like goblets seem,
  All brimming over, one by one,

With ruby drops that catch the fire
   Which, westward, marks the dying sun.

Thus fancy draws with misty lines
   These etchings that I copy now:
" A partridge and a jay-bird's wings,"
   " A squirrel's brush and sumach bough."

SUNRISE

First, one by one, the stars stole soft away,
    And dark and darker grew the western rim ;
    The hornéd moon's bright lustre 'gan to dim,
And then long ripples came of ashen gray
    That tipped the dusky billows of the night
    With myriad trembling flakes of faintest light.

Next, shapeless things new forms began to take,
    A milk-white lance flashed thro' the eastern skies,
    And Dawn unwilling came with drowsy eyes,
All dreamily, as only half-awake ;
    Then slowly rose the sun, a fiery shield,
    And one lone bird-note sounded far afield.

"A Double"

A "DOUBLE"

Low to the east the shadows all are tinged
   With faint, far crimson lines that rise and fall,
Then slowly spread to where the lake is fringed
   With willows, reeds, and rushes brown and tall;
And eastward where the river winds along,
   High up a pair of mallards wing their flight
With outstretched necks and pinions fleet and strong,
   When to the right
Out leaps a double flash of flame through the pale, marshy
     light.

Two quick reports that blend almost in one,
   Two jets of fire that pierce the morning gray,
And the deep echoes, booming, roll along
   The solitary lake and die away.

Like a lead-plummet falls the foremost bird
   Into the waters of the reedy lake,
And as the second sharp report is heard
   The stricken mate, a noble mallard drake,

Strikes his strong wings together as he drops,
    Spins round and round and droops his bright green
        head,
Then whirls down to the water, where he stops
    And floats stone-dead,
While round him scattered feathers lie upon a rippling
        bed.

SUNSET

A CHILL wind blew from the far northwest,
And down through the gates of day it came ;
The sun sank low in a fading glow
And shadows fell on the cold earth's breast ;
The dead leaves stirred, and a last year's nest
Shook, as the winds went wandering by
Through the sunset's flame.

The reeds stood black at the water's edge,
Where the moon's faint crescent lay so still,
And twilight shades from the upland glades
Drifted down over field and hedge ;
The wind sang sharp in the withered sedge,
And a last red gleam flared up and out
From a distant hill.

THE GRAY GOOSE QUILL

I TAKE my gray goose quill in act to write,
But gone are all my thoughts, for echoes near
A clarion-uttered signal strong and clear—
The clanging of the wild geese in their flight,
As down across the wide and star-strewn night
They hold their wedge-shaped course throughout the sere
And boundless void of that bleak atmosphere,
Where swims the moon in garish, ghostly light
And cloudy haze.   Again upon the marsh,
Within the rough-built blind, alert I stand,
And eastward look for the first dawning ray ;
And now, as memory holds subtle sway,
I hear a distant honking, crisp and harsh,
And crush my wingèd pen in clenched right hand.

COBWEBS

A SPIDER spun a gossamer web
With threads of the finest tether,
And as light as the buoyant thistle-down
It swayed in the wind and weather.

And over the threads the breezes swept
As sweet as a fairy vesper,
And over the leaves and the grass below
Came a faint Æolian whisper:

" Oh, I was woven of silken strands
In a web and woof together,
And I swing from a thistle's prickly top
On the brown and wind-swept heather.

" I'm lulled to sleep by the cricket's chirp,
I wake at the skylark's warning;
I am wooed by the twilight's loving eyes
And the tender kiss of morning.

" I hear the chant of the bending trees
   From a distant thicket's cover,
   And faint and far from the sky above
   The cry of the golden plover.

" To-day goes by and to-morrow comes,
   And it leaves me as it found me ;
   I am safe from all destroying hands,
   With the arms of nature round me.

" I care as little for time or tide
   As the fickle wind that passes,
   My world is here with the sun and dew,
   Along with the leaves and grasses."

THE LAST BUFFALO

CHEYENNE and Arapahoe, Pawnee and Sioux,
 Comanche and Kiowa, Blackfoot and Crow—
Their tepees were scattered wherever grass grew,
 Their pony-tracks showed by each river's smooth flow,
And Nature was given them—God the great giver—
 Stream, forest, and prairie with long, rolling mounds,
And there they went forth with the bow, spear, and
   quiver,
 And led the rude chase on those vast hunting grounds.

From dusk Mississippi to where stood the base
 Of the frowning Sierras o'ertopping the clouds,
Upon whose lone steeps the wild sheep found a place
 Where mist wreathed the summits in dim, floating
   shrouds ;
Here lay their domain, no environment bound them,
 Barbaric and cunning, and free as the birds,
And there on the prairies, beyond and around them,
 The buffaloes wandered in numberless herds.

7

Strange cattle who fed on a thousand green hills,
　Cow, calf, and huge bulls with their thick, streaming
　　　manes,
They cropped the rich grass and drank deep of the rills
　In the tortuous streams intersecting the plains ;
And rumblingly there, from the hollow ground under,
　When the mighty mass moved, a low echo began
That wavered and gathered and swelled into thunder,
　While trembled the earth where the buffaloes ran.

And there on their trail the coyote was seen,
　And the greater gray wolf with his glittering teeth,
That flashed from their ambush—jaws narrow and lean—
　As the blade of a bowie-knife gleams from a sheath,
And low in the grass the coiled rattlesnake lying,
　His challenge shrilled out as they swiftly went by,
While mute on the edges grim ravens were flying,
　And buzzards hung over them poised in the sky.

And from their quaint villages prairie-dogs gazed,
　As the endless processions went galloping past,
And over the prairie their pathway was blazed
　As the beaten-down woods mark the hurricane's blast ;
For near and afar the wild flowers and grasses,
　Harsh iron-weed tall and the red roses sweet,

Were tangled and trampled in colorless masses,
  And ground into dust by the buffaloes' feet.

Thus roved the swart bison in days long ago,
  And there the red Indian dwelt by his side,
And there, by the warrior's lance and the bow,
  In hundreds and thousands the buffaloes died ;
And still through the march of the seasons unceasing
  They drifted and mingled and multiplied more,
In dense-thronging bands on the prairies increasing,
  Like the green-bladed grass or the sands by the shore.

But down on their ranks swept the white man at last,
  With his rifle in hand, riding westward for gold,
While hordes of hide-hunters came following fast,
    More fierce than the wolves that had trailed them of
      old,
And the wide Western steppe was an altar of slaughter,
  And the stain of those days with dark mammon abides,
When the rivers ran blood and when blood ran like water,
  For a million of buffaloes slain for their hides.

And there in the sunshine the ravens flew down
  And perched and sat silent on ominous bones,
Grave kings of destruction, sans sceptre and crown,
  Who mockingly ruled from their ossified thrones ;

For out through the distance, far spreading and reaching,
　　As white as the wings of the seafaring gulls,
The horns and the heads of the bison lay bleaching
　　And made of the land a Golgotha of skulls.

The tepees have vanished, the savage moves on ;
　　From the graves of his chiefs to the slow sinking sun,
The realm that he owned to the stranger has gone,
　　And the day of his race, like a story, is done ;
And safe from the clutches of sordid-souled schemer,
　　Far hid in some nook of the mountainous lands,
Black-browed and defiant, and sad as a dreamer,
　　Alone in his might the last buffalo stands.

WINTER

FENCES half buried in the drifting snow,
And trees beside them, ghostly-limbed and drear,
Where wailing breezes wander to and fro
Across the gray and icy atmosphere ;
No sound to comfort and no hope to cheer
Where skies so blank monotonously stare,
While Ceres waits, all dreamy with despair,
And mourns the saddest season of the year.

Leaf, bud, and blossom—flowers—ay, and song
Of warbling birds, all gladsome things like these
In other lands and other climes belong ;
Sun-flooded sands that wait by summer seas,
Green-bladed grass, and leaves upon the trees—
Yet all this will be here, but in a breath ;
For this is sleep—that foolish ones call death—
Till Nature rises from her bended knees.

HUNTERS

A CRICKET fed on an insect
  Too small for eye to see,
A field-mouse captured the cricket
  And hushed his minstrelsy.

A gray shrike pounced on the field-mouse
  And hung him on a thorn,
And a hawk came down on the cruel shrike
  From over the waving corn.

And a fox sprang out on the red-tailed hawk
  From under a fallen tree,
For bird and beast, by flood and field,
  Of every degree,

Prey one upon the other ;
  'Twas thus ordained to be.
My rifle laid old Reynard low,
  And death—death looked at me.

The Rod

THE ROD

A ROD for bass and wall-eyed pike
  When over sandy shoals they throng,
Adapted both to " cast " or "strike,"
  Of split bamboo and lithe and long,
With pliant tip that wavers like
  Some shivering aspen slim and strong.

And at the butt the clicking reel
  With braided silken line is wound,
A miniature of fortune's wheel
  When a good fish the lure has found,
And in your nervous grip you feel
  Its shining circle whirl around.

A good plain rod by all that's fair,
  And whips the water like a thong,
In Northern lakes all lonely where
  The muskalunge and bass belong ;
Supple and straight beyond compare,
  And worthy of a better song.

A "RISE"

UNDER the shadows of a cliff
Crowned with a growth of stately pine
An angler moors his rocking skiff
And o'er the ripple casts his line,
And where the darkling current crawls
Like thistle-down the gay lure falls.

Then from the depths a silver gleam
Quick flashes, like a jewel bright,
Up through the waters of the stream
An instant visible to sight—
As lightning cleaves the sombre sky
The black bass rises to the fly.

OUT-DOORS

A WOOD-CHUCK sat on an orchard knoll,
Brown and still in the soft spring morning,
A martin sprang from a sand-bank 'hole
And a rain-crow uttered his note of warning ;
While down by the creek the rushes swayed
And a nameless pungent music made.
That came and went at its own rude pleasure,
The faint-heard notes of a marshy measure.

A robin piped with a note as sweet
As a flute-note played in a mellow minor,
And the leaf-harps, swept by the breezes fleet,
In whispering tones came fine and finer,
While close by the side of a bulrush bed
A snapping-turtle raised his head.
And a swallow dipped to the creek in passing,
His shadow there for an instant glassing.

A pickerel lay by an old log bridge,
Where the moss grew low on the midmost panel,

He cocked his eye at a passing midge
And waved his fins as he watched the channel,
While a gathering murmur slowly welled
And into a sibilant chorus swelled,
And a tall blue crane in silence listened
Where the long creek-shallows glanced and glistened.

A bobolink rose in the sun-thrilled air,
A spirit of song, with the blue sky o'er him,
And his trembling wings from the meadow there,
As he sang and sang, still upward bore him,
While high where a banner of cloud-film trailed
A hawk, a speck in the zenith, sailed,
And dew on the coarse swamp-grass was clinging,
With Pan's wild chords in the distance ringing.

SPEARING

WHERE a long, narrow channel stretched,
Mid lily-pads and bulrush beds,
And water-spiders slid across,
Like acrobats, on tense-drawn threads,
A pickerel, like a floating log,
Lay motionless within the bog.

And slowly up the channel's tide
A skiff came creeping, foot by foot,
While light as dips a swallow down
The oarsman in the ripples put
His short, broad blade, and bubbles dripped
And smoothly from its edges slipped.

And virile in his vigorous pose
The spearsman in the vanguard stood,
And poised within his raised right hand
The heavy shaft of pitch-pine wood,
Whose iron trident glittered bare
And coldly in the warm June air.

Smooth, soft and smooth, and noiselessly,
The skiff approached the bulrush bed,
And suddenly across the stream
The frightened fish like lightning sped ;
But ere he reached the reeds he sought,
In that one instant, danger-fraught,

The spearsman's arm had straightened out,
The heavy shaft like javelin flew,
It clashed against the ripples there
And lent the wave a ruddier hue,
And on the barb's dull iron gray,
Transfixed, the struggling pickerel lay.

MARSH ECHOES

WHEN twilight on the rushes falls
And threads the moon through night's dark halls,
When dims the far horizon line
And glow-worms phosphorescent shine,
Then comes in deepest basso full,
Like bellowing of a roving bull,
   " Ah-rr-ooomp ! Ah-rr-ooomp !
    Ba-aa-rroomp ! "

O'erhead the ghostly night-hawk flits,
And in the woods in silence sits
The whippoorwill, while round the lake
Soft on the shores the ripples break,
And sound there is none save that call,
Reverberating over all,
   " Ah-rr-ooomp ! Ah-rr-ooomp !
    Ba-aa-rroomp ! "

The tinkling cow-bells in the hush
No more are heard, and in the lush

8

And coarse swamp-grass the bull-frogs lie,
While echoes far their guttural cry ;
A'cross the lily-pads and cane
A solemn and a hoarse refrain,
      " Ah-rr-ooomp ! Ah-rr-ooomp !
         Ba-aa-rroomp ! "

And Pan, among the sighing reeds,
When night has told her starry beads
One after one, stands silent there,
While float upon the darkening air
Those unmelodious, mournful notes
Sent upward from Batracean throats,
      " Ah-rr-ooomp ! Ah-rr-ooomp !
         Ba-aa-rroomp ! "

FISHING

With hickory switch and linen twine
   He sits upon the country bridge ;
Below him, where the sun's rays shine,
   Across the water glides a midge ;
The cat-tails to the ripples tip
   And craw-fish mould their cells of clay,
And wandering swallows downward dip
   An instant there and then away.

Beside him is the homely can
   That holds the bait, and by his side
His yellow dog, a rataplan,
   Beats on the oaken timbers wide ;
Slow swims the cork and then it drifts,
   And bobs and sinks and wavers there,
While bends the switch as quick he lifts
   A wriggling sun-fish through the air.

The meadows ring with melody
   From rapturous fluttering bobolinks,

And on a blackened fallen tree
   Is stretched, as solemn as the sphinx,
An old mud-turtle's awkward form,
   And dragon-flies above him skim,
Out, where the sunlight dances warm,
   And in where shadows hover dim.

I grant you all you else may claim
   When manhood seeks its fullest due,
I grant you honor, place, and fame,
   I grant that she you loved was true ;
I grant you gray in years, and rich,
   So that you but could give me then
The brook, the fish, the hickory switch,
   And time to be a boy again.

THE BROOK TROUT

How swift and strong its waters glide—
The brook—a clear, resistless tide,
And slowly down the mountain side
    The angler goes.
The soft air drifts through solemn pines
And dreamily the sunlight shines,
As past the alders, rocks, and vines
    The current flows,

Above the depths that now conceal
What tempting lures may yet reveal,
An instant whirls the nimble reel,
    Then drops the fly,
And by the glancing ripples caught,
A moment there the line is taut,
And then, as suddenly as thought,
    Goes whirling by.

And where the swift brook turning trends,
Just as the broadening ripple ends,

There comes a tug, a thrill that sends
    Along the rod,
A message from the slender tip
From whence the liquid diamonds drip,
That violently makes it dip
    And downward nod.

And then it bends from tip to butt,
While through the pool the ripples cut,
And close and closer yet is shut,
    Then upward flies,
As drawn from out his pebbly hold,
Brightly against the forest mould,
Vermilion, silver, black, and gold,
    The brook trout lies.

"Broke Away"

"BROKE AWAY"

Out flew the line; the burnished reel
   Gleamed brightly in the waning sun,
The waves lapped lightly 'gainst our keel,
   The day was wellnigh done;
Faint outlined on the southern sky,
   A yellow sickle lay the moon,
And eerily arose the cry,
   Far shoreward, of a loon.

Then bent the rod; the slender tip,
   With one quick curve the silence cut,
Sharp as the motion of a whip,
   Until it neared the butt;
Full well was strained the silken braid
   By swift retreat and sudden tack,
At last one furious lunge was made
   And then the line lay slack.

Then all at once the slackened line
   Stretched outward through the waters deep,

We saw a flash of silver shine,
    We saw a black bass leap ;
By Hercules ! a gallant fish—
    One spring, and like dissolving spray,
The line and, leader parted—" swish "—
    Click—" broke away."

DIANA

BARELEGGÈD to her shapely knee,
   She waded in the mountain brook ;
To her an infant's A B C
   Was every leaf in Nature's book ;
And in her brown and lithe left hand
   An Indian bow she lightly held,
While up from 'neath her tangled hair
   Her eyes like clear spring water welled.

Over her shoulder round was flung
   A quiver of long arrows keen,
And there she trod the rocks among,
   A wild and graceful forest queen ;
And often on the ripples came,
   A sight she marked with eager eyes,
Sharp rushes, marked by bubble-rings,
   Where the trout rose to snap at flies.

And whiles she set a feathered shaft
   Close to her cheek and drew the bow—

Well skilled was she in forest-craft—
    And smiled to see her arrow go,
As flashed its point against the stream
    Like lightning, where the ripples shook,
Transfixing in his downward rush
The finned chameleon of the brook.

MINNOWS

THE minnows through the water slid,
Pellucid shadows, vague as dreams ;
And darting o'er the pebbles hid
Safe in the shore-line's yawning seams.

An instant there, as morning beams
Flashed from Old Sol's half-opened lid,
The minnows through the water slid,
Pellucid shadows, vague as dreams.

Round a huge bowlder of the streams,
A gray, half-sunken pyramid,
Like sudden flight of pallid gleams
The brook's transparent depths amid,
The minnows through the water slid,
Pellucid shadows, vague as dreams.

THE DESERTED BOAT

DEEP in the soft black ooze it lies
Slow rotting under summer skies,
And over it the blackbird flies.

The sand-snipe skim across the space
Where the old boat finds resting place
Close folded in the weeds' embrace.

Sun, sun and shadow, wind and rain
Come following in the season's train
And mark its form with many a stain.

Along its lines the ripple sleeps,
Upon its bow the turtle creeps,
And by its side the pickerel leaps.

And one lone lily, white and gold,
That seems a touch of hope to hold,
Gleams bright against its blackening mould.

THE REDWING

On a bulrush stalk a blackbird swung
All in the sun and the sunshine weather,
Teetered and scolded there as he hung
O'er the maze of the swamp-woof's tangled tether ;
And the spots on his wings were red as fire,
And his notes rang sweet as Apollo's lyre.

The summer woods were a haze of blue,
Draped and robed with an emerald kirtle,
And the blackbird whistled clear and true
Till the thrush was mute in the flowered myrtle ;
And the spots on his wings were red as fire,
And his notes rang sweet as Apollo's lyre.

A black bass leaped for a dragon-fly
And struck the spray from the sleeping water,
While airily, eerily, there on high
Sang the blackbird pert from his " teeter-totter ; "
And the spots on his wings were red as fire,
And his notes rang sweet as Apollo's lyre.

A fig for the music born of man,
I shake my head and I doubt me whether
Your cultured strain has a charm for Pan
When a blackbird sings in the sunshine weather,
With the spots on his wings as red as fire,
And his notes as sweet as Apollo's lyre.

A "Strike"

A "STRIKE"

A RIVER winding through the marsh
Where rushes waver crisp and harsh,
And slowly by the farther shore,
With softest sweep of dripping oar,
A boat goes past along the edge,
By lily-pads and matted sedge.

And in the stern a figure stands
With fishing-rod in outstretched hands,
And where the line is outward cast,
Near to the rushes drifting past,
All brightly 'neath the morning beams
The trailing spoon-hook swerves and gleams.

Then suddenly the lithe rod bends,
And swift the tense, taut line extends,
As all at once from watery lair
A watchful pickerel lurking there
Drops like a panther on the prey,
Strikes, feels the hook, and darts away.

"Pine-sheltered shores"

"All noiseless, comes a long birch-bark canoe"

THE DEATH OF THE MUSKALUNGE

PINE-SHELTERED shores that stretch 'neath northern skies,
And under them a dreaming forest lies;
Dim shadow-trees, whose moveless branches stand
Like castle-turrets in a sunken land.

And gliding o'er the lake's smooth-mirrored blue,
All noiseless, comes a long birch-bark canoe,
And in its bow a sun-bronzed fisher kneels,
While from his rod, with outward motion, wheels

Swift in the air the glimmer of a "spoon,"
Curving a crescent like the pale new moon;
It strikes the surface with a liquid sound
And through the water, shining, whirls around.

Then all at once a mighty fish upsprings,
The rod bends double and the bright reel sings,
As from the depths a giant muskalunge
Vaults and evanishes with sullen plunge.

And once again from out the emerald deeps,
Shaking his jaws, the great fish upward leaps ;
Then 'mid the ripples furiously he goes,
While after him the light canoe he tows.

Another bound, and like a sounding flail
He slaps the water with his lusty tail,
And as he stretches at the silken reins
The tough rod quivers and the tackle strains.

An hour's passed since first he took the "spoon,"
And wanes the day to deepest afternoon ;
Long, dusky curves bask silent on the sands,
Darker below the buried forest stands.

Up from the shades he struggles once again,
A desperate rush—a feebler one—and then,
Conquered at last, he rises from the shoals
And, half inert, upon the water rolls—

Yields to the gaff, and soon the noble prize
Before the victor unresisting lies ;

The contest over and his strong race run,
A battle royal by the sportsman won.

Westward the sun with flaming distaff twines
A blood-red garland round the tufted pines,
And day, slow sinking in the ruddy light,
Sees gray stars blossom by the paths of night.

The Death

VALE

HE was an old-time friend of mine—and one to trust ;
  We followed the streams as comrades, with rod and
    gun,
  And together we roamed the hills in rain or sun ;
But now he is gone, and all that is left is a handful of
    dust.

The out-door man, after all, is the one with heart,
  For it cramps the body and soul to live in-doors ;
  In out-door-land the spirit high as an eagle soars,
And his was an eagle spirit, though now it soars apart.

Music he heard in the winds and the running streams.
  In the rifle's sharp report and the thunder's peal ;
  In the thrush's song. in the click of a winding reel :
But now he is silent in death, that last great dream of
    dreams.

Friend and comrade of mine by wood and marshy shore.
  Thine absent self on me a subtle power wields ;

Thou art with me still by the rivers, lakes, and fields,
Though the lakes and rivers and fields henceforth know
thee no more.

Thou art above me now—beyond the azure dome,
Of the far blue heavens whose void will ever be
Between our paths as a soundless, shoreless sea,
Till a cry from the dusk shall stay my steps and call me
home.